The

We live in a very unequal world. One kind of inequality is especially hard to talk about, that's the gulf between the few people who are distinctively good-looking and the majority of us who are by comparison, not.

But we don't normally feel there is anything we can do about it, there isn't anyone to get angry with. It's just something you learn to deal with, growing up I would have settled for just average-looking. I've heard it said many times, that life is what you made it but I believe people and your upbringing

Tributes a lot to how your life turns out I

know mine did.........

Chapter One

I have offend wondered if maybe my real mother had left me when I was only two years old, because I wasn't the idea baby she had hoped for, what reason would a mother have to walk

Away from her child, after all wasn't a mother's love support to be unconditional. Growing up with my Dad and step mom, I never experienced the affection that a child has with their parents, I never heard the words I love you from either of them, I had always been on the scared side of my stepmom, I looked at her as Cinderella looked at her stepmom because growing up I was treated about the same way, as a young boy as soon as I came home from school, I would have to clean the house make the beds, before I was allowed to go outside, I guess I didn't mind as much as I should have , it was just the way of life for me.

Many years later at her funeral it's sad because I couldn't make myself cry.

When I was in my twenties, I had written my real mom a letter asking her why she left me and why she never tried to come see me, since we lived in the same town, she didn't answered, but her daughter did write me back, making excuses for her mother, but I knew the truth, she never loved me or wanted to see me.

I worked hard to gain the attention of my father and I always seem to fail at each try.

Growing up, My Step-mom's sister and her five children would come and stay with us, it seemed many times.

I was very jealous of the relationship that my dad had with the other kids, because he treated them so differently then he treated me, I would watch as he played around with them, they received the attention that I craved, but never got. It made me feel like I was just an unlovable kid.

I think if I could have experienced some kind of affection from

My dad, my life growing up might have been slightly different.

In school from as far back as I can remember, I was very insecure about the way I looked, and there was never a shortage of the name calling from the other kids. But the only thing I could do was come to terms with the fact that I was a homely kid and all the tears in the world were not going to change that fact.

I remember when I was in second grade. I was chasing a boy in our classroom just playing around, he tripped over a wooden chair, and his foot came up and knocked my front tooth out.

Because I guess I needed one more thing for the kids to make fun of.

I got called a lot of names growing up, and despite the name calling, I did have friends in school, I even had a girlfriend

through grade school and because I was the tallest kid in my class, the name calling seemed to stop in my own classroom, I think because we had mostly all grew up together, and they had come accustom to the way I looked. But the older kids in the higher grades still gave me a hard time. And the new kids that came to our school that didn't know me, would make fun of me, I never let the kids know what theirs words did to me, I just took it and went on with my life, after all there wasn't much I could do about it. I always knew I had a big nose and the

Older kids never missed an opportunity to call me Gonzo, a name I had to live with, because it came from not only school kids, but friends and family

I don't think they ever considered that their little remarks bothered me, because I became good at hiding my feelings.

I learned to join in on the laugher at my own expense because it was easier for me to hide my hurt then to show it.

I just held on to the old saying "Sticks & stones can break my bones, but words will never hurt me" but the truth was, the words hurt me more than any stick or stone possibly could.

Chapter Two

I went to a little country school where the grades were in one class room. When I entered into sixth grade, our class room held the sixth grades, seventh grades and eight grades. I felt like I was the teacher's pet, he would always put me in charge, if he had to leave the classroom for a few moments, I would write down the names of the kids that talked, and if I had to tell them not to talk I would write my own name down for talking as well, {I took my job very seriously}

the school only went to the eighth grade so after I left and stated school in another town, I really got ridiculed for the way I looked, I knew I was a good person on the inside, but unfortunately people can't see your insides.

My sixth grade teacher from my old school and his wife came to all of my games. It gave me a good feeling to know someone came to watch me play.

Chapter Three

My Dad was never home when I was growing up, he would come home after work, eat supper and leave, and not come home until bedtime, I felt like I grew up without a father or a mother, I always felt like I was used by

Both of them, I was just a convenience to have around, especially for my step-mom, I was her little slave boy, to clean and run errands for her.

I knew my dad didn't love my stepmom and on weekends he would use me for an excuse to go see his girlfriend, pretending to be taking me to get a haircut, or whatever, I never could understand why he stayed with my stepmother, so I just came to my own conclusion that he was scared of her, I know I was, she was a big woman with a very loud mouth, she intimidated a lot of

People, including my Dad.

She had never showed me any kind of love, even though she had raised me since I was just two years old.

She was just my stepmother, she loved my dad, and I was his son.

The only person I have ever felt love from was my grandmother on my real mom's side, I never seen my real mom who didn't live far from me, guess she had better things to do, but I was happy I got to spend time with my grandmother, she always treated me special and I know she felt bad because her daughter deserted me.

I spend a lot of Saturdays at her house

that was my happiest times growing up as a child.

I was very hurt when she passed away, I felt like I had lost the only person that truly loved me.

Chapter Four

When I was around thirteen, me and some other kids were in the back of a truck at my cousin's house, I watched a girl with long brown hair walk out of the house, carrying a baby, I remember thinking how pretty she was, and I watched her for a long, right up until we drove away.

I wasn't really into girls at that age manly because I was into sports so much, it hurt me sometimes because my dad never came to my games, I was proud of the way I played soft ball, but I didn't have anyone to share my excitement with when we would win a game, I just kept my victory to myself.

My dad would get drunk a lot, and I can remember lots of times going with my stepmom to pick him up from a bar.

I looked at my dad as kind of like a rebel without a cause, through the years he never seem to want to better his life, I guess he was either content or very unhappy.

When I was fourteen years old, I went deer hunting with my dad. I was sitting on the ground and my heart started to hurt, at first it was a mild pain, but as time passed the pain kept getting worst. I went and found my dad; I told how my heart was hurting. "What does the pain feel like?" he wanted to know.

"I don't know, my heart just hurts and it is getting worst" I didn't know how to explain it to him.

"You stay right here, I'm going to go find Steve." He told me. We started toward the hospital but first he dropped Steve off at his house. I heard him tell Steve to call my mom and tell her we were picking her up.

I wasn't scared because I really didn't understand what was happening to me. But once at the hospital, they ran tests and told us I had a heart attack, he also said if I had been in my sixties I would be dead right now. God spared my life that day.

Through the many tests that followed,

I was told I could never play sports again.

I missed a lot of school because of my heart.

But as the time passed, I didn't listen to my Doctor and I started playing softball, on a church league. Something I had really enjoyed and I just didn't want to give it up.

Chapter Five

The following year I got a job at a steakhouse. I started out as a dishwasher, it wasn't long before I became a cook, I liked my job and of course I got some little remarks like I did at school but I still made a few friends.

When I turned seventeen, I dropped out of

school and worked full time. I worked there for three years then I got a factory job, it only took me three months to become a supervisor. It was there I met Helen, she took a liking to me and was constantly wanting me to meet her daughter,

I was pretty sure after finding out my age and we both agreed her daughter was too young for me, that the Subject would be dropped, but it wasn't. Sitting at my desk one day at work, Helen came up to me.

"Eddie I know I said that you were too old for Emma, but I really like you and I know you would be good for her, I have talked about you to her many times and she wants to meet you". With those words she

dropped a piece of paper on my desk and said "She is expecting your call" and she walked away with a mischief smile on her face. I picked up the paper and seen it was her phone number, I all at once became nervous at the thought of calling her, I was kind of on the shy side, and I spend the rest of the day going over in my head what I could say to her.

Once at home, I had already gone over a thousand different conversations in my head, I almost felt like I had already talked to her. I toyed with the piece of paper until I got up the nerve to dial the number. We only talked for a few minutes, we made plans to meet the next night at her job, she worked at Pete's pizza, which was a children pizza place with games and live characters.

The next day I wanted to look my best so I went out and purchased new clothes,

I was nervous when I walked in, but I was soon to find out it was for nothing because she chickened out, I should have known.

I took a seat, but not knowing what she looked like I just sat and watched the employees, which was two guys and an older woman but I did get a little annoyed at a few of the characters, that kept coming to my table.

So I got up and walked out, I went through

a drive through to grab something to eat and went home to call it a wasted night.

A few nights later I did talk to Emma again, she had in fact chickened out but not the way I have thought.

She said she was too scared to meet me so she had dressed up as one of the characters I could understand that.

So again we make plans to meet at her work, but this time she wasn't dressed as a character, when she got off of work we went outside to sit in my car and we talked I really liked Emma, and I had no idea there was a plot already turning in her pretty little head.

After that night I hung out with Emma a few more times, but I could tell the potential of something developing with us was not there, Emma showed no interested in me that way. That's why two weeks later when I was given the opportunity to be transferred with my job to Texas, I took it. I needed a change in my life, to go someplace new and make and save some money, get ahead in life, in my mind I had it all figured out I would someday come back home move out of my parent's house, maybe buy my own place and get a good job.

Chapter Six

I Will never forget that day, my truck was packed, and I was ready to take off and start my new life.

When out of the blue, my dad said he loved me, the first time in my life I had ever heard those words from him it touched me, looking back on it now,

I wonder why it was so hard for him to tell his only son that he loved him?. I never heard those words again from him.

I found an apartment and started to help Sit up the factory where I would be working as a supervisor. Even though Emma didn't seemed to want a relationship with me when I was around her, that all changed once I moved to Texas. We now talked on the phone almost every night, and I was beginning to develop feelings, I knew I probably shouldn't.

After a little while being in Texas, I met a guy at work and started to hang out with him, at first we just would stop at a bar after work, which beat going home to an empty apartment, but then the drinking started to get a little heavy, and after a while when I wasn't at work I was at a bar drinking, and it seemed like all my money was going for alcohol, and all of my plans weren't even on the horizon anymore.

I think I came to realize this when on a Friday evening, I went to the bar and slept Saturday completely away, a day I had told my fellow employees to show up for work. I woke up Sunday morning thinking it was Saturday, only to find no one was there, I was very upset that not one had showed up for work.

The next morning I just hung out at my apartment or I should say down by the pool, my apartment was too depressing with no furniture in it.

Monday morning they would be hearing from me about not coming to work on Saturday.

I not knowing at all it was indeed Monday. So you can image how foolish I sounded when I showed up for work on Tuesday morning, jumping on to my employees for not showing up for work on Saturday, when it was me who hadn't showed up Saturday or Monday, and they were not afraid to expressed this to me.

I knew it was time to go home before I turned into an alcoholic or something even worst.

After given my notice at my job, I was headed home with lots of regrets, but I knew I only had myself to blame, I had to be the one to change my life, but I let my life change me.

Chapter Seven

It didn't take me long to get another job, my plans were to only stay with my parents until I got on my feet and got an apartment, and that time came sooner than I thought it would. I was still talking to Emma, and she started to beg me to get an apartment with her because she knew her mom would never allow her to move out on her own

And she took advantage of the fact that her mother liked me, and she knew she would allow her to get an apartment with me, even though I knew this, I still felt like her feelings had changed toward me, and there may be a future in the making for us. I fooled myself into believing that, right up until the day she introduced me to her new boyfriend, and then I knew she had just used me to get out of her mother's house.

I wasn't mad at Emma, just a little hurt but I knew I couldn't stay there in the same house with her and her boyfriend,

Even though I did really like him, he was a nice guy.

One night she decided to introduce me to her friend, I was sure it was because she felt guilty for leading me on, and using me. The first night I met Kelly, we just sat and talked the whole night, I wasn't attracted to her I guess I was just sick of being alone. I decided to move out and find me another place to live, there were too many parties going on with teenagers, and I didn't want to be involved in that.

I talked to Kelly every night on the phone and the first time we went on a date. Her mom dropped her off at my house. We went out to eat and back to my house, only to discover her parents moved all of her things into my house, they have kicked her out. Looking back on that day now, if I could have seen my future, I would have left the outline of my body on the wall like a cartoon character. And ran for my life. But unfortunately life doesn't work that way.

We make mistakes. Then we live in that mistake and then we suffer the consequences of our mistakes.

So Kelly moved in with me, I wasn't happy about it, but I didn't know what else to do. The truth was I was a shamed to be seen with Kelly because of the way she dressed, she ran around showing half of her body, she dressed and acted very provocative, and it was an embarrassment.

It was about two months later I was at work, I decided I had enough, I was at a dead end job, that I hated, I had no feelings for Kelly and I just wanted out of my circumstances.

So I did the only thing I knew to do, I quit my job that day and decided to leave my apartment and move back in with my parents. But my fate had a different idea.

When I pulled into the driveway, Kelly was sitting on the steps. "What are you doing home?" she asked.

"I quit my job" she just looked at me before she said the words I will never forget. "Eddie, I'm pregnant." I'm pretty sure all the blood ran to my face. Even though I did not love Kelly or want to spend the rest of my life with her, I knew I had to do the responsible thing and it was now my obligation to take care of her, I knew there was no actual connection between us. But I made my bed so whether or not I liked it I had to lay in it. I had no idea at that time that Kelly was just a ticking time bomb that would explode as

soon as she got the marriage license, and in her warped mind think she would own me, and I would have do whatever she said or face the consequences. And believe I would face a lot of consequences. I wish I would have known that marriage was going to be a very negative outcome.

Chapter Eight

It wasn't long before my money started to run out, so we had to find another place to live, I couldn't go back to my parent's house because my mom hated Kelly. So we stayed a few nights here and there with family and friends.

One day we were out driving around and I

saw a friend walking so I stopped and gave him a ride, we talked, and I told him our situation.

"Take me to my factory, I'm sure I can get you a job there" he said. So that day I got a job which was a big relief to me

I had a friend that didn't live from my new job, so I asked him if we could stay with him just until I got enough money to rent our own place. He wasn't working at the time.

So I talked to my new boss and I also got him a job there.

We worked the same shift, when we came home, his wife would have his dinner cooked and waiting for him.

I would have to cook mine and Kelly's dinner, I can honestly say I had never met anyone as lazy as her, I could tell his wife was getting fed up with us being there and I knew I would have to quickly finds us a place to live before we wore out our welcome.

I didn't blame my friend's wife because I knew Kelly didn't help do any house work or cooking.

But it took six months, before we moved into a house not far from my parents.

I was ashamed for people to come over, because of the way our house was always so messy, she never did dishes so there were always dirty dishes everywhere. and it just got worst after our daughter was born, she didn't have a lot to do with the baby, while I was at work, Kelly's mom would come over and stay and take care of the baby and clean our house, and I would take care of the baby when I came home from work, Kelly said she was going though postpartum depression.

When our daughter was 12 days old Kelly and I got married because I thought that was the right thing to do.

But I soon learned sometimes doing the right thing is not always the right thing.

The night before the wedding Kelly had spent the night with her mom.

I had a friend and my half brother over; we ordered a pizza and drink a six pack of beer two beers *each.*

The next day after the wedding we came home and she seen the empty beer cans and went ballistic and started to break every things in the house.

I just stared at her in shocked, this was over six empty beer cans.

She was acting like because now we had a marriage license that she could control my every move, and after that day, that is exactly what she tried to do.

I felt like I had just entered the portals of hell.

But I knew it was me that had opened the prison door and walked in freely.

Hunting was my passion, it was my place of non-reality and escape, I could be alone and give my head a chance to clear and relax. But then one year Kelly tried to even steal that little enjoyment that just came once a year.

She insisted that I let her go hunting with me. my first reply was a big fat NO, but she wore me down with her constant begging and pleating, so one day at work after getting off the phone with her,

I started coming up with my own little way of teaching her that she couldn't take this away from me like she had took everything else, if she wanted to go hunting, than she can go hunting but I was going to make it as hard and as miserable on her as I possible could.

As strange as it sounds I kind of enjoyed myself, I took her through swamps, and walked her through briers, I didn't wait for her, so she had to hustle to stay up with me. She never asks to go hunting with me again.

Chapter Nine

The first of many red flags to appear was whenever I didn't immediately jump to her command, she would get mad and scream, she would throw things, it was like living with an out of control chimp. I never knew from one moment to the next what she was going to do.

Kelly still hung on to the story of having postpartum depression.

She would lay in bed all day naked, while her mother took care of the baby when I was at work.

I never could understand why she refused to wear clothes, I became accustomed to Kelly's screams and little fits; I would just ignore her which seems to make matters worse.

I came home from one day and she was out of bed and dressed.

After that's She even started to attend church with her mother.

I went a few times; but only because they had a softball team and I wanted to play on their league, after about month going there, the Pastor talked to me about moving and driving a cab for him, it sounded like a good deal, he was also going to give us an apartment to live in so I took the job. I was still looking for that change in my life and still making mistakes.

So we moved there and I started driving a cab, it was a tourists town and I picked up and dropped off a lot of people at the beach, and because of this, the fighting began to get worse with Kelly, she was so Jealous I was going to pick up girls from the beach, and whether I did or not, I was accused of a lot more than just giving them a ride in my cab, I was so sick of her accusations. Living with Kelly was almost like listening to someone speaking a different language, haft of the time I could never understand what she was talking about, how could she not understand that driving a cab, I might have to pick up and drop off girls.

At the end of the month, my boss tried to charge me rent for the apartment, we were living in. Even though I knew it was a part of the agreement, he said it was not a part of the deal, so I quit and we moved into a trailer and my old boss gave me my job back. I was very unhappy with my life and I felt trapped in a loveless marriage with no hope out, the constant fighting and accusations was tearing me down little by little. It felt like I was caught in a whirlwind of chaos, with the life being sucked from me. It was nonstop crazy arguing with her every day, about stupid things that were out of my control.

Chapter Ten

One night I had a nightmare, I dreamed I was at a funeral and I looked around the room and spotted the widow standing with another woman I assumed was her mother and she was weeping.

And so much anger hit me.

I dreamed I walked up to her and in a very

loud voice I said "you did this! You did to this to him!" I was so mad I just wanted to punch her in her face, but instead I turned and I looked at the casket and it was me laying there and when I turned back around to the widow, it was Kelly. I woke in a cold sweat.

I can remember one night, she wanted to go to a drive inn movie, and we took Sara to my mom to babysit. When we first got to the movie and found a parking space, we both went to the concession stand and got drinks and food. So about half way into the movie, she tells me to go back to the concession stand to get her something else, I asked her very polity because I knew I had to choose my words very carefully as to not make her mad, if she could wait until intermission. At first she didn't say anything she just went back to watching the movie, and I breathed a sigh of relief, and continued to watch the movie also, the next thing I knew she poured her drink all over me and then she jumped out of the car banging the car door as hard as she could, she looked at me like Satan, her eyes had so much angrier in them, I actually got scared, then she opened the door and slammed it closed again. I put the speaker back on the hook and started the car; I was going to drive away whether she was in the car or hanging on to the door, I knew this behaver was crazy and when I look back on my life with Kelly, I realize I was also to blame for letting her get away with the things she did to me.

I didn't really know how a to deal with what was going on, I hadn't had a serious relationship before, but I could now see this was a sign of the beginning of abuse, but I guess I was just naïve. I should have known this kind of marriage was a long-term effect on our mental and emotional state of mind.

She was so hypocritical it was actually unreal, she would be screaming at me throwing things in the house, and then Answer the phone in this sweet little innocent voice that would make me stand there with my mouth hanging open.

I remember when I first got with Kelly, she told me that she'd never stay with someone who treated her badly, no matter how much she loved them, yet she expected me to take all the abuse from her. And I did. Most of my family and friends couldn't stand Kelly;

they told me she controlled me.

So I just started hiding the abusive, I felt like a loser, but the truth was I didn't know how to get out of my predicament.

I didn't physically have the evidence on the surface, of an abusive marriage but my character showed the scars of her Controlling.

I felt like she was actually gradually destroying my life.

Chapter Eleven

I had invited a longtime friend of mine and his wife to our house one evening to play cards. They were Christians, so you can image my shame when my crazy wife got mad because she was losing at cards and started cussing and throwing her little tantrum, I could tell they were embarrassed I didn't know if they were embarrassed for themselves or for me, they immediately got up and left. She had made a fool of herself and of me.

I was on a softball team and I can remember one time we were playing for second or third place in state championship we had two out we were down a run in the last inning. I'm a left field hitter, I have never hit to the right field before. The coach on the opposite team pulled all the players to left field so that left right field wide open, I hit a line drive right down first base line all the way to the fence I ended getting a triple which brought a guy on third base home, and tied the game. The next guy hit a single, which brought me home; we won second place.

in state championship. Later the coach came up to me and told me, "I've never seen you hit the ball to right field, I'm so glad you have the ability to do that. It felt good to get praise for my playing.

When I played softball I put of my problems aside.

Sometimes I just thought of my life as being on hold for a little while,

so instead of facing my problems and doing something about it, I would just blame it on the fact that I was raised by a woman, who used me and yelled at me and I still felt like that scared little boy.

I didn't know or learn how to face confrontation. I had been put down and made fun of my whole life and in a hostile situation, so I guess it just became easier for me to accept the things the way they were instead of doing something about the situation.

Even though I knew I was putting myself in danger.

Like the one night, Kelly woke me up beating me, she was on top of me hitting and scratching me, and I knocked her off and jumped up. To this day I still don't know why?

But that's why I started working eighty hours a week, I even slept at my job sometimes, because it was better to work then be at home with the constant fighting, she would call me at work, mad and screaming, and sometimes show up and embarrass me in front of my coworkers, by making a big scene, everyone by now knew she was crazy. I was constantly asked the same question by many people "Why didn't I leave her?" but in my mind, I always had the intentions of leaving one day. It's not like I wanted to stay in this miserable marriage and I knew getting a divorce should have been a no-brainer you might think. But in my mind there were so many factors to consider, but the degree of my "misery" itself. Should have been my only factor. I had often wondered why Kelly didn't want out. Was it possible that she was also miserable in this marriage and not completely aware of it.

Chapter Twelve

Ever Since I was thirteen I had been collecting old cars, and I had a big collection, I had them on display and was very proud of them.

One day I came home from work to find them all broke and smashed up;

I didn't say anything, what was the point? She must have packed all the broken parts up and saved them because a few years later she had her brother fix them back up and she wrapped them as my Christmas gift and gave them to me,
I threw them in the trash. There is no reason, or emotional understanding with a crazy person.

Sometimes I felt like I was suspended in time, and I would wake up and realize my life has been nothing other than just a bad dream.

One evening we went out with another couple, against my better judgement, because I knew how she acted when she had an audience, and she didn't disappoint me.

She ordered me to wear my seat belt like I was a child, I refused because I knew it wasn't for my safety but the fact that she would use every available tactic to gain control. By the time we got home I was humiliated and she had turned into Sybil...

We moved again into a bigger house and while I was away deer hunting, she moved her brother and his wife into our house.

So there were three people living there that did not do any kind of cleaning, after a while the house became so bad, I got a big trash bag and just started picking things up and throwing things away. I hated my life.

I told her brother he had to start paying rent, he didn't like that idea so they moved out and I was glad.

The fighting between Kelly and me got worse and worse, so she wanted us to see a marriage counselor so instead of arguing about it, I agreed. The day he came to our house she met him at the door and after she introduced him to me, she walked out and got into her car and drove away, while we just stood there wondering what had just happened. He looked at me and asked "Where did she go?" "I have no idea" I said. "Well I needed to talk to both of you".

I apologized for wasting his time. I knew why Kelly left it was because she thought this was my entire fault and she hoped the marriage counselor would straighten me out, but the truth was, he probably thought she was just as crazy as I knew she was, she made a fool of herself.

If there could have been a way to resolve our disagreements seemingly before they happened maybe it could have saved me a lot of embarrassment.

We didn't go out much, because I never knew which split personality Kelly would end up with, before we made it back home. She always went out of her way to embarrassed me when we were around people. She would constantly interrupt me, run over me when speaking, or completely ignore what I had to say, so I figured it was just easier to stay home.

One day a friend had come over because I was getting a ride to work with him, but Kelly had her own ideas and she didn't want me to go to work that day, I tried explaining to her I couldn't miss work but she wouldn't listen, so I just walked out and got into the truck and we both watched as she tore the screen door down and threw it to the ground.

Chapter Thirteen

It had been quite a roller coaster ride with several different things, too many too mention.

I remember one day she wanted to wallpaper a door way up the stairs and because of the angle she wanted wallpapered I was having a hard time making the wallpaper stick, which frustrated me, so I started outside to take a break and to get some fresh air before I tried again. "Where are you going "she demanded"; "outside I need a break" "So are you going to finish this?" She stood between me and the door way, "Yes I just need a break" I said trying to stay calm. "You are not going outside, I want you to finish this job now!" she demanded in her (I'm getting angry voice) Because she wasn't going to let me pass, I just grab the door and pulled it off the hinges, knocking her to the floor in the process...... I just needed out. After I cooled off, I put the door back on, trying again to pull the door off of the hinges, just to see if I could, but I couldn't pull it off.

Another time during one of her crazy fits she threw a picture frame at me and I threw it back and it stuck in the wall right beside her head.

I had asked myself what I was still doing here.?

And I knew it was because of my daughter.

But I knew we couldn't just go on like this because someone was going to get hurt.

Chapter Fourteen

One day I was sitting in the living room watching television, I didn't know we were fighting, because haft the time I didn't know.

The next thing I knew there was a gun pointed to the back of my head and she pulled the trigger thankfully the gun wasn't loaded, I quickly jumped up and she was pumping it again, she had no idea the gun was not loaded.

I took the gun away from her and then I packed up all of my guns and took them to my dad's.

I think it really hit me that day that I was living with a lunatic.

And every day she proved it more and more that she was crazy.

We attended a family reunion and my cousins that I hadn't seen in a long time hugged me.

When we got back home Kelly threw a fit accused me of sleeping with my cousins, she got so angry she tried to stab me with a knife. I felt like I was walking in a field of landmines.

A few days later, she came home from church and said to me. "We are going to a marriage counseling seminar in Detroit for the weekend; the church is paying for it." Nothing I wanted more than to be in a hotel room with a crazy woman, but I have learned it is easier to just go along with her idiotic ideas then to fight with her and pray that one day she would say to me...."We have an appointment with a divorce lawyer."

After we checked into our rooms we were told to meet downstairs for our first class, something I wasn't looking forward to.

It turned out not to be that bad, after he talked for a little while, he sent us back to our room to write down things about what we got out of his message and did we learn anything from his talk basically about our feelings on the subject.

And we were to return in an hour.

But just before we left to go back to the class, Kelly looked at me and without reason said.... "The girls you work with, I don't want you to talk to them anymore"

I said "Well that's going to be kind of hard since I'm the supervisor and I don't know sign language " "You think this is a joke, but I'm serious, I forbid you to speak to them again ever!" she screamed at me. I closed the room door and went and sat back down, I no longer wanted to go back downstairs to the class because I knew she was going to humiliate me in front of those people,

about twenty minutes into hearing her screaming at me, the phone ringed. "Hello" I was thankful for the interruption. It was the counselor. "Hi, is everything okay up there?" He asked.

"No it's not" I said. "Okay, should I come to your guy's room" he asked. "Yeah and you probably should bring help" I told him.

The counselor and his wife came to our room and I told them why she was mad. "I'm a supervisor at my work and I was just informed by Kelly that I was never to speak to the women that I work with again, and I tried to explain to her I have to talk to my employees it is my job" all the time I was talking to them I had to almost scream so they could hear me because she was again going ballistic on all of us, I sat for over two hours while

They tried to calm her down explaining to her I had to talk to women because it was my job and how unreasonable she was being, and that she was putting me in a very difficult predicament, and how she should trust me.

I knew all the talking in the world would not change her, I also knew it was my fault too because I never showed her any affection but I felt like she has killed any passion that may have been there, and now I was just at the point I didn't care because not only did I not love her, and I didn't want to work my marriage out,

I just wanted out of it. I didn't even like her because of all the things she had put me through.

It was like she would to try to find any weaknesses in me and then she would focus on that until she brought me down.

I don't think she wanted me to have any happiness at all in my life, she couldn't stand to see me enjoying any aspect of peace at all, and she was very good at her job, because I was definitely man most miserable.

They left our room saying they would see us in the morning.

The next morning instead of going to class we left and went home, we didn't speak all the way home which was fine with me. Silent was definitely golden for a while anyway.

Chapter Fifteen

Everyday became unreal, she would not let up on me not talking to the girls at work, same argument over and over I started spending more time at work because I was almost scare to be home I didn't know what she was capable of doing,

I knew it wasn't a marriage counselor we needed, but that she needed a psychiatrist.

The arguments grow in intensity over time, and often escalate into verbal or physical abuse.

One day I came home from work and she had cut up all of my underwear and then demanded I take off the ones I was wearing and when I refused she tried to cut them off of me, and ended up cutting my leg. She was convinced in her mind that I was sleeping with every girl at my job. My life was a nightmare. But it wasn't nothing compared to the day I came home from work and she wanted me to strip down so she tell if I had cheated on her that day. This was my crazy life , I just pushed past her and went into the kitchen to fix me some dinner while she screamed and kept demanding for me to do it. and because I wouldn't give in to her insanity request that made me guilty of sleeping around on her.

I felt like I was trapped inside a cloud of disbelief and doubt, I only knew one way of escape, and that was to get as far away from her as possibly, but I didn't make that move soon enough. I woke up one night to find her holding a knife to a part of my body I will not mention. I just laid there frozen, scared to move until she put the knife down then I knocked her off the bed. And pushed her out the door and locked it, she screamed and banged on the door until the wee hours of the morning.

The next day I brought padlocks and moved into the spare bedroom.

Every time someone would come to our house she would act like she was in control of me, but what she didn't know was that no one liked her because of her controlling attitude among other reasons. I had so much resentment in me because of her craziness and insanity behavior.

I remember another time I had went fishing with a friend and while we were there another friend and his girlfriend showed up, we were all sitting there, when Kelly walked up and seen the girl there, and even though the girl was sitting with my friend and I was far away from them, it was just the fact that a girl was there, so she started screaming at me and accusing me of being with this girl. I was so embarrassed,

I just wanted to jump into the water and drown myself.

My friends would witness how Kelly treated me and they just couldn't understand why I didn't just punch her, or put her in her place, and believe me many times I have wanted to , they have no idea how many times I had to resist the urge. But we all know I would be the one who's arrested, because women are more commonly the victims of abuse.

Chapter Sixteen

Kelly could never keep a friend, as long as you were her friend, you were never allowed to have other friends and as soon as they found out how she really was, they would stop talking to her.

I remember one time a family moved in across the street from us and Kelly made friends with the woman, which I was glad because it took the focus off of me for a while, until one day I came home from work, the two of them were sitting at the table talking, I didn't speak to either of them, I walked into the bedroom to change my clothes, Kelly came in and sat on the bed.......

"You think I'm stupid don't you?" she said.

"What are you talking about? I never said you were stupid" I already knew where this going, I thought her friend had left, I had no idea, she was still in the kitchen,

and probably could hear every words that was said.

"No you didn't say I was stupid, but you may as well, because you act like I am, you don't think I seen the way you looked at her? you know Eddie, if you want to sleep with her, I will go ask her right now! Is that what you want?" " Kelly, don't be crazy, I didn't look at her in any way" I was starting to get very upset, I was too tired to be fighting with her today
She stormed out of the room and I could hear her screaming at that poor girl,
"Did you know my husband wants to sleep with you? Did you know that? Or have you already slept with him?

Because of Kelly's loud mouth, I couldn't hear what the girl said but I did hear the door open and close" I was glad she left. I just stayed in my room for the rest of the night,

We never saw that girl again. To her and her family now, we were probably just the crazy people that lived across the street. Kelly was Suspicious of every girl.

I had just finished making supper and I carried my plate into the living room to watch television while I ate, when I heard her screaming at me for some unknown reason, I looked up just in time to see she had a big butcher knife in her hand and was coming toward me, I dropped my plate and ran out the door, I didn't go back that night I slept in my neighbor's car and stayed low, I could have stayed in my truck or went to my parents, but I was scared she would find me. It seemed like every single day, it was always something with her and I never knew the signs, it was like one second she was fine and the next she was a mad woman, definitely a Jekyll and Hyde situation going on in her head.

Everything had to go like she wanted it to go. And she expected everyone to do exactly what she said, especially me.

I got up one morning for work and while I was taking my shower, she came into the bathroom to tell me I wasn't going to work that day, she needed me to stay home. It was too early to jump into her crazy mind so I said nothing and with my silence she figured she had made her point and I wouldn't be going to work, but it had never entered my mind not to go to work, the truth was I looked forward to going to my job just to get some peace.

As I was about to walk out the door she started screaming like a mad woman... "What kind of man would leave his wife and daughter home alone with the window broke out?" she screamed... "What are you talking about? There is no window broke out" as soon as the words were out of my mouth, she picked up a kitchen chair and broke the front window out. She had to be in control at all times, but not this time, I walked out the door.

No one understand how my life was with Kelly because I didn't go around telling everyone I live with an abusive wife, I know this whole thing might seem even more bizarre because I'm a man. But men experience partner abuse as well, my family and friends only knew what they saw, but they didn't live with us, and for me to say my life with Kelly was a living nightmare is putting it very mildly.

I was trapped in an emotionally abusive relationship and, every day, I felt like I was fighting a losing battle.

Our daughter spent a lot of time at my parent's house which I was glad because she didn't need to be around her mother when she would get all crazy.

Every day there would be door-slamming, screaming meltdown over the most trivial little things. And she doesn't seem to care who's around to witness it either.

I knew things couldn't continue as they have been.

Another memory I have took place a couple of weeks before I left.

I met Kelly and her sister and her husband for dinner.

I got to the restaurant later than everyone else and as I greeted them both, Kelly burst out laughing.

"So what so funny?" I asked as I sit down.

"Your funny" Kelly said....

"I watched you as you came in, checking out every girl here, I thought your eyes were going to pop out of your head, that's why I was laughing, because you are hysterical, thinking any of these ladies here

would ever have anything to do with you, you make me sick" she finished with a laugh..

suddenly I seen her for exactly for what she was... a nasty obnoxious, offensive, showoff brat, an evil person, and I knew that something had to change because I couldn't stand the site of her, it was her that made me sick.

So I stood up and told her to find her own way home and I left.

Because tonight I had decided not to roll over and play dead.

I stayed away for two nights, she called my parent's house at least a hundred times, but

I Just kept hanging up on her, I know now

I shouldn't of went back but I did.

Chapter Seventeen

The very last straw was the day I came home from work and she was rearranging the living room furniture. I started helping her, she got mad at the way I was helping and started Screaming at me, and the couch was about four feet from the wall she charged at me with a knife, I punched her in the chest, she flipped over the couch and fell up against the wall. I walked out and never walked back in, I knew if I didn't leave I would end up dead or in prison.

If life has taught me anything, it's that sometimes cutting ties with a toxic person is the best thing to do for yourself.

Especial with those who are not good for your mental health, or in this case physical health, either? But I should have known I would never be free of Kelly, she would continue to make my life as miserable as she possibly could. I had to always be on guard.

She became my stalker, she followed me everywhere, she would come to my job going nuts on everyone it was humiliating, she became my worst nightmare.

One day I was sleeping upstairs at my parent's house I opened my eyes to see her right in my face, I screamed, she scared me to death, she was constantly begging me to come back, she was driving me in sane, why couldn't she just go away and leave me be, I told her this many times, I also told her I would never go back with her it was over. Why would a prison return back to his cell once he was free?

And the funeral dream scene plays in a loop in the background of my brain all the time..

I can't even imagine ever going back with her, not ever.

I knew I was going to have to live with this mistake with Kelly for the rest of my life, its funny our minds have a sneaky way of justifying our actions so that we never have to feel like we did something stupid.

Chapter Eighteen

Kelly would not let up on me, it seemed like every corner I turned she was there, she came to my job, sometimes in a screaming fit, one day she destroyed my office, the ladies in the offices couldn't stand her, everyone was starting to see exactly how my life had been living with her.

There was a day when I was at my apartment, I didn't hear her come in the front door because I was in the back room lifting weights, I looked up to see Kelly and her new boyfriend standing there. When I put the weights down and got up from the seat, Kelly laid down on the seat and picked the weights up, showing off in front of her boyfriend I'm guessing, but the weights were to heavy and they were down across her neck, I stood there laughing as I watched her friend try to left the weights off of her, when he finally got them off of her she looked at me and said..."You were going to let me die, wasn't you?"

She was constantly showing up at my apartment or at my parent's house uninvited trying to have a conversation with me. I knew because she was always in control of everything, that now it was beyond her logic; to understand she was no longer in control.

Another time, she caught me off guard by her unexpected visit, she came over and started to beg me to take her back, and go to yet another marriage counselor, I was so tired of fighting with her, so I made an agreement with her, I told her I would go, only if she would agree to leave me alone and get out of my life afterwards. She agreed.

Chapter Nineteen

I Agreed I would meet her at the church where the free marriage counseling was to take place.

After the introduction, we went down to the basement, the pastor asked who would like to go first, and I said I will... I began to tell him everything that Kelly had done to me Kelly was sitting there crying, while I talked, but I wasn't moved by her tears. When I had finished telling of the many horrible and shocking things she had did to me in just the short time of our marriage, and the reason I had to get away from her. He looked at her and said did you really do all these things? She said "yes" he said "I would hate your guts." I will never forget his words and I will never forget the shocked look on Kelly's face when he said that to her, her plan backfired, she was hoping if I came here, the pastor would set me straight, but instead the pastor gave her the hard cold truth, that she could not get away with treating people the way she did and expect them to want to be around her, all I knew is I wanted far away from Kelly as I could possibly get, and the only communication I wanted with her would be concerning my daughter only.

I asked the pastor, "Are we done here?" He said, "I think we are" I walked out,

She followed me to my car. "Are you happy?" She asked. "Yes I am and I hope you keep your promise and stay away from me" I got into my car and drove away.

The times I was with Kelly I had always had a feeling that because she knew I had no self-esteem, and I did feel worthless and

I think she never thought I would actually leave her, because I didn't have a better option or I couldn't find anyone else, so I was stuck with her, and that is why she was having such a hard time accepting the fact that I would rather be alone for the rest of my life than to be with her.

I don't know why it took me so long to leave her. I knew her behavior wasn't normal.

And I had always felt the need to escape before it was too late,

I guess you could say I was embarrassed to admit that my wife was abusive for fear of being judged, like it was my fault. In the beginning I thought it was, because I had gotten her pregnant .

I thought I was being somewhat noble, but I didn't know also that it was a foolhardy decision that would cost me years of unhappiness.

I wish I would have had someone to talk to me back then, and tell me how to avoid a bad situation altogether and if I married Kelly that the probability was that I was only going to make a bad situation worse.

I know now that I did make it worse by marrying her and doing what I thought I should do, rather than what would have been best in the long run.

The day she told me she was pregnant; I knew she wasn't right for me.

Chapter Twenty

I Knew I would never truly be rid of Kelly because we did have a daughter together and that made it more complex, I told her without hesitation what was going to happen in the future. She was never to call me unless it's an emergency or something related to our daughter. I knew

I had to set some boundaries with Kelly, if not she would continue to try to control my life.

Every other weekend when it was my time to have Sara, I would have Kelly dropped her off at my parent's house, so I wouldn't have to see her, my parents adored their granddaughter, and she adored them.

I tried to move on with my life. I was invited to a friend's wedding and not wanting to go alone I asked another friend {which was a woman} but still just a friend that I worked with to go with me. I picked her up and brought her back to my apartment so I could get dressed, and then we would leave from there. I was in my room getting dressed for the wedding, when Kelly came over. I heard my friend talking to someone, so I walked out to find Kelly screaming, demanding to know who this woman was and what she was doing here I made Kelly leave. We were now divorced and she had to comes to terms with the fact she could no longer just come to my apartment and tell me what I could do. My life was now my own I no longer had a prison warden to answer to.

Every time Kelly would drop Sara off, she would always have to come in with her new boyfriend and visit.

One night I got a phone call from the police, telling me to come to the police station and get my daughter, because Kelly was in jail, I wasn't surprised at anything this woman might have done. I found out that she had broken into some guy's house and broke and cut up his things.

I had no intentions of giving Sara back to her once she got out of jail, but she begged and pleated with me to give her daughter back, she promised she would change, and feeling like my daughter deserved to be with her mother, I let her take Sara back.

I was very happy when Kelly remarried. I thought at last she could be someone else's problem. But unfortunately my luck don't go that way, she still went out of her way to make sure my life was miserable.

I started to party and hang out with friends I enjoyed my new found freedom, I felt like I had been let out of prison.

Kelly was divorced from her second husband he had experienced the same things I had and he divorced her because he wanted to live.

She had come to my parent's house to drop off Sara, and I was there with a girl, and she threw a fit, even though it had been six years since our divorce.

I dated a few girls, but nothing serious. It's funny, because even after the horrible nightmare marriage I lived in, I still wanted to be married just to the right person. I had always wanted a son, because I was a hunter, I wanted to pass that skill down to my son, and I hoped one day, to remarry and be happy in my marriage. But if that should never happened for me,

I was still very happy to be out of a toxic marriage, at least now I have hope of surviving, being with Kelly I didn't see a hope. I had always told people I would die before I was thirty, and I believe whole heartily if I hadn't got away from her when I did, I would be dead today.

But I now look back and feel stunned that I actually got to a point in my life where I was scared of her, Like she may kill me while I was sleeping or take me by surprise one day.

By that point in our relationship,

I felt worn down from constantly having to anticipate her changing moods.

That was my life thirty four years ago... And I have learned that we do live in a small world because that young girl I saw when I was only thirteen years old, sitting in the back of that pickup truck at my cousin's house, we have been happily married for 21 years...........

Made in the USA
Monee, IL
17 May 2020

31268527R00079